# THE CLUE IN THE SHADOWS

Look for these books
in the Clue™ series:

# THE CLUE IN THE SHADOWS

Book created by A. E. Parker

Written by Jahnna N. Malcolm

Based on characters from the Parker Brothers® game

A Creative Media Applications Production

SCHOLASTIC INC.
New York Toronto London Auckland Sydney

*Special thanks to: Diane Morris, Sandy Upham,*
*Susan Nash, Laura Millhollin, Chris Dupuis,*
*Maureen Taxter, Jean Feiwel, Ellie Berger,*
*Greg Holch, Dona Smith, Nancy Smith,*
*John Simko, Madalina Stefan,*
*David Tommasino, and Elizabeth Parisi*

ISBN 0-590-48934-8

12 11 10 9 8 7 6 5 4 3 2 1                  5 6 7 8 9/9 0/0

Printed in the U.S.A.          40

First Scholastic printing, February 1995

*For Dona Smith*

# Contents

# THE CLUE IN THE SHADOWS

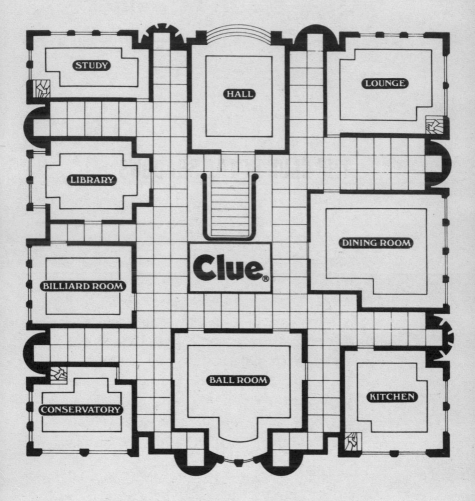

# Allow Me to Introduce Myself . . .

**I**'m Reginald Boddy, your host for this evening's bash. Pardon me for asking, but would you mind whispering? You see, I'm having a dinner party and my five guests and my maid are in the Dining Room slurping the remains of tonight's soup. I don't want them to know I've tiptoed into the Kitchen to sample this evening's dessert, baked Alaska. It's simply scrumptious!

That reminds me — the last time I snuck into the Kitchen, I almost didn't make it out alive. These same guests were visiting for the weekend and when I stole off to sample the pie, Miss Scarlet, ever the life of the party, swung at me with her Lead Pipe. Luckily for me she missed, but the Lead Pipe hit the edge of the pie plate, which flipped through the air and knocked me out. I don't remember what happened before or after that, but the guests must have had a good time, because — as you can see — they're back.

Could I ask one more small favor of you? Would you mind keeping an eye on my suspects — I mean, my maid and my guests? It seems like every time they visit, something truly criminal occurs. The suspects are:

Colonel Mustard: a gallant, sporting sort of fellow. Unfortunately, his favorite sport is fighting duels, so I'd stay on the sidelines if I were you.

Mrs. Peacock: What can you say about this prim and proper lady? Whatever it is, be *very careful*, or she'll think you're rude, rude, *rude*!

Mr. Green: A fine businessman. Rumor has it that some people have called him a big bully. (Unfortunately, they didn't live to tell about it!)

Miss Scarlet: This ravishing beauty's favorite color is red. She loves it so much that she even *sees* red (especially when she doesn't get her way).

Professor Plum: The ultimate absentminded professor, Plum has the brain of a genius (which he keeps in a jar in his laboratory).

Mrs. White: Ever cheerful and faithful, my charming maid has seen me through many disasters. She's seen me fall out of the Conservatory window, and I'm fairly certain she saw Miss Scarlet try to bean me with the Lead Pipe in the Kitchen.

Confused? Don't be. At the end of each chapter, a list of rooms, suspects, and weapons will be provided so that you can keep track of the goings-on at Boddy Mansion. (I myself will never be a suspect, of course!)

"AAAAAAARGGGGGH!"

Speaking of goings-on, I think I heard a blood-curdling scream coming from the Dining Room.

Excuse me, will you? It appears Mrs. Peacock has some complaint about her meal.

# 1.
# The Bug Stops Here

"AAAAAAARGGGGGH!"

Mrs. Peacock's bloodcurdling scream fairly shook the windows of the Dining Room. However, none of the other dinner guests seemed to notice. They were too busy arguing about the origin of warthogs with Professor Plum, who was seated at the head of the rectangular dinner table.

Mrs. Peacock screamed again, her face turning the color of her royal-blue silk suit.

"What in heaven's name is going on?" Mr. Boddy shouted as he raced into the Dining Room.

Mrs. Peacock clutched at her throat and pointed at the bowl in front of her. "There's a bug in my soup."

Mr. Boddy peered over her shoulder at the soup bowl. Smack dab in the middle of the clam chowder was a big, black beetle with six shiny black legs and two long antennae. "By Jove, you're right," he said, trying hard not to gag at the gruesome sight. "That *is* a bug. A very large bug, I might add."

Mrs. Peacock sat stiff as a board, her face frozen

in a look of complete repulsion. "Please, Mr. Boddy, take it away," she murmured. "Get it out of my sight."

Before her host could make a move, Professor Plum, who was seated to the left of Mrs. Peacock, grabbed him by the arm. "Warthogs are from North America! Mr. Boddy will agree with me, won't you?"

"Well, I've never really thought about it," Mr. Boddy replied.

Mr. Green leaned across Mrs. Peacock's soup bowl from his place on her right and barked, "Warthogs are from Middle Europe. I'm certain of it."

Miss Scarlet fluttered her long tapered fingers, the nails of which were dotted with bright points of red polish. "The warthog is cousin to the hedgehog," she cooed from her place at the opposite end of the table from Plum. "And I believe the hedgehog originated in Africa."

Mr. Green, who was sitting to Miss Scarlet's left, raised his soupspoon to his lips, murmuring, "That's a lie."

Colonel Mustard heard Mr. Green from his place on Miss Scarlet's right. He pointed his spoon menacingly at Green and snarled, "Are you calling the lady a liar? I challenge you to a duel."

Realizing that tempers and soups had reached the boiling point, Mr. Boddy quickly intervened. "The encyclopedia will settle this once and for all,"

5

he announced. "I have a set in the Library. Shall I go look?"

"Allow me," Professor Plum said, dabbing his lips with his napkin and scooting back his chair. "You sit down and finish your soup."

"Nobody seems to care that there's a bug in my soup," Mrs. Peacock whimpered to the table in general. "This is so rude."

"Stop sniveling and let me have a look," Miss Scarlet said, finally paying attention to Mrs. Peacock's cry. She hurried around the table to her. "I'll dispose of that bug for you."

Mrs. Peacock squeezed her eyes shut and shuddered. "Ugh. It's so big."

"My word!" Miss Scarlet gasped as she got her first glimpse of the insect. "It is huge, and extremely ugly." But when Miss Scarlett picked up a large soupspoon and started to fish the bug out of the clam chowder, she made another discovery. "It's also plastic."

"Plastic?" Mrs. Peacock squinted one eye open. "You mean, it's fake?"

"It looks like someone has played a joke on you, Mrs. Peacock," Miss Scarlet giggled loudly.

"Of all the rude pranks!" Mrs. Peacock folded her arms acros her chest and huffed, "I'll just bet it was that maid."

"THAT MAID," Mrs. White replied, suddenly appearing through the swinging door to the kitchen, "had nothing to do with THAT BUG! For

6

your information, I was in the Kitchen slaving over an extremely hot stove."

Mrs. White circled the Dining Room table, picking up soup bowls and slamming them onto her tray. Her starched maid's uniform with its little white apron and matching white cap crackled with each brisk step. Then with a forced smile, she curtsied and marched back to the Kitchen.

"Well!" Miss Scarlet said, slipping into Professor Plum's chair at the head of the table, "She certainly was huffy."

"I don't care if it was plastic," Mrs. Peacock continued, holding her napkin to her mouth. "That bug was very frightening."

"I'm sure whoever did it only meant it as a joke," Miss Scarlet said with a smirk.

Mrs. Peacock lowered her napkin to reveal a tight-lipped mouth. "As you can see, I am not laughing."

"Found it!" Professor Plum called as he returned from the Library. He held up a thick volume in one hand. "The encyclopedia had a very long entry on warthogs. Would anyone care to hear it?"

Seeing that Miss Scarlet was now sitting in his chair, the Professor took hers at the opposite end of the table. He grinned smugly at the guests as he opened the book and began to read. But before he could say anything beyond, "The warthog — " he was interrupted.

"Off! Off! Unhand me, you villain!"

Colonel Mustard leapt up from the table, knocking his water glass and his chair over in the process. He danced in a frenzied circle, hurling his napkin as far away from himself as he could muster.

"Colonel, please!" Mr. Boddy shouted. "Get a hold of your — YIKES!"

Now Mr. Boddy was on his feet, doing the same hysterical dance.

"Help! Help!" the two men shouted in unison.

Mrs. White exploded through the swinging door, clutching a large silver salad bowl and a pair of sterling silver tongs. "What's the matter? Why are you screaming like that?"

Mr. Boddy and Colonel Mustard pointed speechlessly at the floor between them. Lying palm up on the Oriental carpet was a bloody, severed hand.

Mrs. White covered her mouth with one hand, nearly stabbing herself in the nose with the salad tongs. "Ew! Ick! Ouch!"

Mr. Green rose from his seat and leaned across the table to see what all the commotion was about. "Calm down, you fools," he said. "It's rubber. That's a rubber hand."

Colonel Mustard, who was holding his chair in front of him like a lion tamer, gasped, "It's rubber? You mean, somebody played a trick on *me*?" The Colonel's mustache twitched angrily. Still bran-

8

dishing his chair in front of him, he turned slowly and glared at the other guests at the table. "I challenge you *all* to a duel. The entire lot of you!"

"Now, now, Colonel," Mr. Boddy said as he bent to pick up the trick rubber hand, "let's not get carried away. This just seems to be another little joke on all of us."

"Not funny," the Colonel muttered, shaking his head from side to side. "Not funny at all."

"Salad is served," Mrs. White shouted, a little too loudly. She was still smarting from the pinch her nose had gotten from the salad tongs. "Help yourselves."

"You'll have to pardon me," Mrs. Peacock announced, struggling to her feet with her napkin held firmly across her mouth. "This has simply been too much for me. I'm sure I couldn't eat another bite." Mrs. Peacock half-walked, half-ran from the Dining Room.

Seeing that her chair was now vacant, Professor Plum promptly moved over and sat down on it. "Miss Scarlet, even though everyone else seems to have lost interest, I'm sure you'd like to read about warthogs." He spread the open book before her on the Dining Room table.

Ten minutes later . . .

Ten minutes later, the remaining guests had finished their salads and were waiting eagerly for

9

Mrs. White to deliver her award-winning main course.

"Boodles of Noodles," she announced, proudly dishing out a heavy serving of pasta coated in a thick tomato-and-apple sauce on each guest's plate. "Dig in. There's more where that came from."

"Mmmm!" Professor Plum said, sniffing his plate in delight. He smiled at the guest seated to his right. "Smell that aroma."

"Look!" Mr. Green held up his fork. At first glance, a thick strand of pasta appeared to be danging from it. But on closer inspection the guests were dismayed to discover what the object really was.

"AGGGHHHH!" they shrieked. Their forks dropped in unison, clattering noisily against the china. "A worm."

"That's gross!" Mr. Green said, flicking his fork to get the worm off.

"That's disgusting," Miss Scarlet said, tossing her napkin onto the table.

"That's enough!" Mrs. White cried, heaving her apron, hat, and towel at them all. "One of you is trying to ruin my dinner, and I won't stand for it. Do you hear?"

"Are you accusing me?" Colonel Mustard bellowed, leaping out of his chair and glaring at Mrs. White. "If so, I challenge you to a duel."

Mr. Green sprang to his feet and shouted at

Colonel Mustard. "Maybe *you* did it. It's just your kind of humor."

"How could *he* do it?" Miss Scarlet shrieked at Mr. Green. "He found the severed hand."

"Then I say it was *you*," Professor Plum said, picking up the worm from the tablecloth where it had fallen and dangling it under Miss Scarlet's nose. "Because you didn't find a bug, or a worm, or a hand in your food."

Professor Plum tossed the worm at Miss Scarlet, which signaled the onset of a full-fledged food fight. The enraged guests hurled fistful after fistful of spaghetti at each other.

After ducking several boodles of noodles, Mr. Boddy finally put two fingers in his mouth and blew a shrill whistle that made everyone cover their ears in pain.

"Peace, friends, peace," he begged. "These little jokes have been very upsetting, but I can guarantee you that nothing will spoil Mrs. White's dessert."

"Dessert!" the group groaned in unison. "Yuck!"

None of them was about to try eating anything else.

"Who knows what might appear on our plates next?" Miss Scarlet said with a delicate shudder.

"Don't worry about a thing," Mr. Boddy said as he gestured for them all to take their seats. "You see, I know who the joker is."

11

"You do?" Colonel Mustard arched one bushy eyebrow and leaned in toward their host. "Who?"

Mr. Boddy smiled serenely. "I'll give you a hint. In every instance, the trickster was sitting beside the victim. And to be even more precise, the trickster always sat to the victim's left."

## WHO IS THE PRACTICAL JOKER?

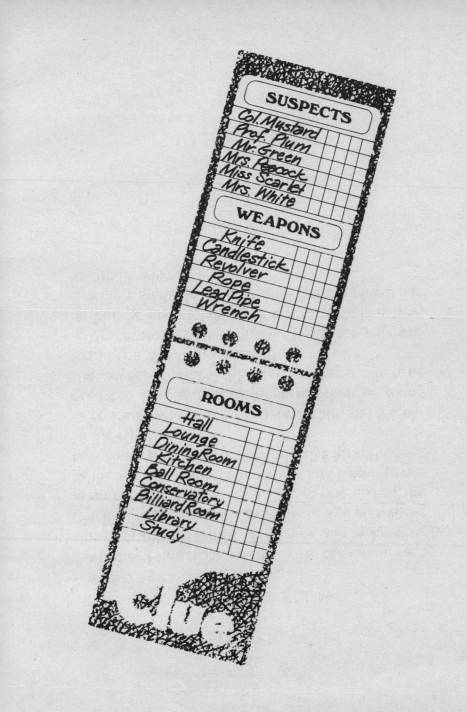

# SOLUTION

## PROFESSOR PLUM

Professor Plum was seated next to the victim each time a prank happened. We know this by keeping track of the seat changes. The original seating arrangement had Miss Scarlet at one end of the table, with Mustard to her right and Green to her left. Plum was at the other end, with Mrs. Peacock to his right.

So Plum was next to Peacock when she discovered the beetle, beside Mustard when he found the severed hand, and next to Green when he found the worm in his noodles.

Unfortunately for Professor Plum, the joke was on him as his friends later put salt in his coffee, a rubber snake in his bed, and itching powder in his underwear.

# 2.
# Read It and Weep

"It's brilliant. Simply brilliant," Mr. Boddy declared. He was standing in the center of the Library, surrounded by his weekend guests who waited eagerly to hear just what was so brilliant.

"I thought of this idea earlier in the week and have waited days to tell you about it." Mr. Boddy clapped his hands together in delight.

"Well, speak up, old man," Colonel Mustard encouraged. "I, for one, am all ears."

"Yes, darling," Miss Scarlet purred, placing her red-velvet-gloved hand on Mr. Boddy's sleeve. "We're all dying to find out about your idea."

"Well, as you know, I love literature." Mr. Boddy gestured to the massive wall of books behind him. "In a good week, I'll devour six or seven books."

"Food for thought, eh?" Professor Plum joked.

"Right. At any rate," Mr. Boddy continued, "knowing that you all love reading as much as I do, I thought we should form a club."

"A club?" Mrs. Peacock stared at him blankly. "You mean, with secret handshakes and dues?

Because if that's the case, count me out. I find all of that nonsense rather rude."

"No, no, no," Mr. Boddy replied with a hearty laugh. "This would be a book club."

"What's it going to cost us?" asked Mr. Green, whose number-one concern was always money.

"Absolutely nothing," Mr. Boddy reassured him. "I'd buy the books. All of you would read them. Then we'd discuss them over dinner once a month." He shrugged and added, "One book a month. That's the beauty of the idea."

At the mention of the word "beauty," Miss Scarlet leaned forward. "I love clubs, Reggie dear. When do we start?"

"As soon as we select the books. I suggest we pick three and go from there."

"The first book should be *The Cracked Code*," Mrs. White announced from her station by the coffeepot. To prove her point, she pulled a Revolver out of her apron.

"Look out, she's got a gun!" Miss Scarlet cried.

In an instant the guests had thrown themselves onto the Library rug.

"Don't be so jumpy," Mrs. White said, waving the gun nonchalantly. She struck a pose like a spy, crouching down and clutching the revolver with both hands. "I just love a good mystery."

"Mysteries are all fine and dandy," Professor Plum said, smoothing his hair back in place as he climbed back onto the couch. "But I prefer science

16

fiction. How about that new Bobby Fineline book, *Galactic Tales from Other Planets*? I hear it's delightful." Professor Plum reached behind one of the pillows on the couch and pulled out a Lead Pipe. He pressed it to his lips and blew on it, making the sound of a rocket ship blasting off. "*BRRRROWWW!*"

Mrs. Peacock stuck her fingers in her ears and muttered, "How dreadfully rude."

Mr. Green, who was standing beneath one of the Library's lighting sconces, suddenly raised one arm. The other guests gasped as the shadow of a large figure wielding a Knife spread across the Library carpet.

"I want to read *Murder at Midnight*," Mr. Green said in a menacing voice. "Everyone should read it. It's a classic thriller."

"I don't want to read anything too scary," Miss Scarlet said, her red lips puffed into a pout. "And you can't make me."

Mr. Green lowered his arm and tucked the Knife back into his breast pocket. "Dull, that's what you are," he grumbled. "D-u-l-l."

"Well, if it's excitement you want," another guest said, suddenly leaping onto a leather footstool and spinning the Rope above his head like a lariat, "nothing beats *The Last Roundup*."

"Unless it's *Kiss and Tell*," breathed Miss Scarlet, holding up her lit Candlestick so that her face was bathed in a soft, romantic light.

17

"I find those types of books vulgar," said another guest, who tugged at her skirt to make sure it covered her knees and checked her high-buttoned sweater to make sure it came to just under her chin. She reached in the purse that she clutched on her lap and pulled out a Wrench, as a warning to any who might come too close to her. "I prefer *The Long and Drawn-out Life Story of Esther Keefoover.* I hear it's seven hundred pages long. It could take us months to finish."

"Months?" Mr. Boddy gulped. "I think the idea is that we should read a new book every thirty days."

The guest with the Wrench shrugged. "Then you'll just have to stay up late and remain at home on weekends to finish it, won't you?"

Mrs. White was standing right behind the guest with the Wrench and stuck out her tongue at her. The rest of the guests felt like doing the same.

Not wanting to be accused of playing favorites, Mr. Boddy quickly proposed a plan for selecting the three books. "We'll have a drawing. I'll write Mystery, Science Fiction, Western, Thriller, Romance, and Biography on slips of paper and then put them in a hat."

"May I be the one to pull the papers out of the hat?" Miss Scarlet asked, fluttering her long eyelashes at Mr. Boddy.

He made a quick check with the other guests,

then shrugged. "I don't see why not. You will draw three slips of paper from my hat, and those will be our three types of reading material."

They waited anxiously as Boddy wrote the categories on pieces of paper and dropped them in. He handed the top hat to Colonel Mustard, who shook it vigorously. Then Mr. Green held the hat while Miss Scarlet made the first selection.

"Biography," she read to a chorus of groans.

Miss Scarlet reached in the hat a second time and handed Mr. Boddy the slip of paper.

"Our second book will be a mystery," announced Boddy.

Mrs. White, who was refreshing Professor Plum's cup of coffee, squealed with glee, nearly spilling the hot liquid in the lap of a dismayed Mrs. Peacock.

Miss Scarlet closed her eyes and took a deep breath, determined to make the third choice be hers. But when she reached into the hat and pulled out the paper, Mr. Boddy announced, "It's a thriller."

"Yes!" Mr. Green, who was not usually the demonstrative type, surprised everyone by doing a little dance of victory across the Library rug.

After they had finished their coffee and dessert, the guests retired for the evening. They took their weapons with them, of course.

No one was completely happy with the results

of the book drawing. In fact, nearly all of the guests had reached the decision that the book situation called for drastic measures.

Thirty minutes later . . .

Thirty minutes later, the guest with the Rope and the guest with the Candlestick met in the Kitchen to devise a scheme.

And the mystery lover and the thriller lover met in the Library to concoct a plan of their own.

Both pairs arrived at the same conclusion: "The biography lover must die."

That way a new book subject could be chosen for the club.

That night . . .

That night, the Kitchen team crept into the biography lover's bedroom, carrying their weapons. The guest with the Rope whispered, "I'll just slip this around her neck, and pull."

"Whatever you do, be quick about it," the other guest hissed. "It's drafty in this old barn of a mansion and I want to get back to bed."

Just as the guest with the Rope was about to strangle the biography lover, the bedroom door creaked open. The Library team stuck their heads into the room.

"Yikes!" the guest with the Rope gasped. "Let's get out of here. Through that window, quick!"

"Not on your life," the other guest whispered. "It's cold and nasty outside. Let's hide. Follow me."

They disappeared into the closet, just as the Library team tiptoed into the room.

Unfortunately one member of the Library team stubbed her toe on a chair by the foot of the bed and howled in pain. "Oooh, that smarts. Owie, owie, owie."

"What's going on?" a voice mumbled from the bed. "Who's in my room?"

"She's awake!" both team members gasped, throwing their hands in the air. Unfortunately for them, their weapons flew over their heads and hit the floor behind them with two loud clunks. Two more clunks followed as both guests fell to their knees and groped around in the dark, trying to retrieve their weapons.

"Who's there?" the voice demanded from the bed. "Speak up, or I'll call the authorities."

"Give me that weapon," an angry voice rasped. "It's mine."

"I'm keeping it," the other voice hissed back. "Because you've got mine."

The intruders, each now holding the other's weapon, stood up just as the biography lover reached for the light switch.

BANG!

21

A shot rang out and the biography lover slumped to the pillow, dead.

## WHO KILLED WHOM? WHERE? WITH WHAT?

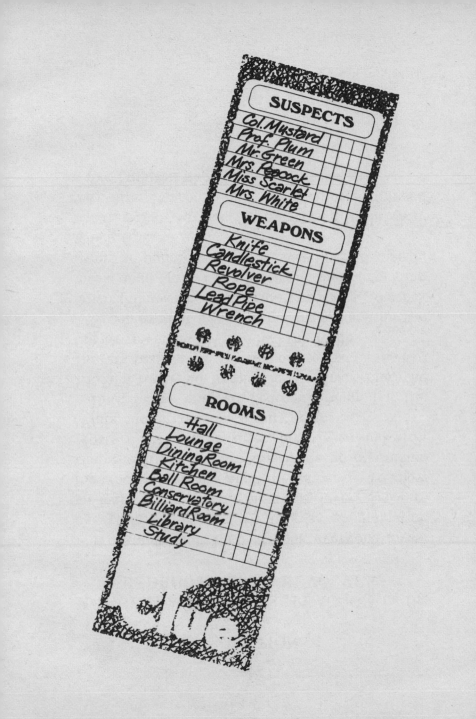

# SOLUTION

MR. GREEN killed MRS. PEACOCK in the
BEDROOM with the REVOLVER.

We know what kind of book everyone loves,
except Mrs. Peacock. By process of elimination
we learn that she is the biography lover. By keeping track of weapons and types of books, we know
that the Kitchen team was made up of Colonel
Mustard and Miss Scarlet; Mr. Green and Mrs.
White comprised the Library team.

Both teams entered Peacock's room, but the
Kitchen team hid in the closet. Meanwhile, the
Library team switched weapons so that Green had
the Revolver and White had the Knife.

Green fired at Peacock, but missed and hit the
down pillow. The shot frightened Mrs. Peacock
into a dead faint. Luckily, the feathers exploding
from the punctured pillow caused her to sneeze,
which revived her.

After that, to make up for trying to do away
with Mrs. Peacock, everyone was forced to read
a five-hundred-page biography of *her* choice.

# 3.
# The Guys in Disguise

While cleaning the attic of the Boddy mansion one day, Mrs. White made a startling discovery.

"A trunk! A huge, leather steamer trunk!"

Mr. Boddy was in the Billiard Room when he heard her shouts from above. Hurrying to the foot of the attic steps, he cried, "Mrs. White, is everything all right?"

Mrs. White appeared at the attic door, a feather duster in one hand and a can of Dust-Away in the other. "Mr. Boddy, I've just discovered an extremely large trunk. It was tucked under one of the eaves, hidden behind a secret panel."

Mr. Boddy's eyes widened. "I wonder, could it be . . . ?"

He took the attic steps two at a time and leapt into the room. Mrs. White flattened herself against the doorway so he could pass. "What are you talking about?" she asked.

"Uncle N.E. Boddy's trunk of theatrical costumes," Mr. Boddy cried. "It was shipped here when I was a young boy and then one day, it just disappeared."

Mrs. White waved her rag in the direction of the western eave. "It's over there. But why would someone put four padlocks on a trunk full of moth-eaten costumes?"

Mr. Boddy wove his way quickly through the narrow passage between the piles of storage boxes and sheet-draped furniture. Then he laughed with glee. "It *is* Uncle N.E. Boddy's trunk. It is! Just think, it was right here under our noses, all this time. And I never knew."

"Do you think he left any money in there?" Mrs. White asked. She hoped what she had found was a treasure chest filled with gold coins and jewelry. And that there would be a reward for the trusty servant who had discovered it.

"Good heavens, no," Mr. Boddy chuckled. "Uncle N.E. was as poor as a church mouse. But he certainly knew how to have a good time. Here, Mrs. White, help me take this downstairs."

Mrs. White clenched the handle of her duster between her teeth and bent to pick up the heavy trunk, muttering, "I rish I'd nebah fond dis." Which, roughly translated, meant she wished she'd never found the trunk.

They lugged the trunk down the attic stairs, through the upstairs corridor, and down the grand staircase into the great Hall. Mrs. White dropped her end abruptly and, taking the duster out of her mouth, said, "Could we take a breather, please?"

Mr. Boddy patted her on the back. "You've done a fine job, Mrs. White. I'll get Green or Mustard to help me carry this the rest of the way."

Mr. Green had just lost his third game of snooker to the Colonel and was eager for some new diversion. He helped Boddy carry the trunk to the Billiard Room where the rest of the guests were still gathered.

"What's in this trunk?" Mr. Green puffed as they carried it to the center of the room. "It weighs a ton."

"A lifetime of theatrical costumes," Mr. Boddy replied, excitedly. "My great-uncle N.E. Boddy was a master of disguise. Years after he quit the theater, he'd appear at our door in costume. We'd never recognize him. One year he'd be an old gypsy woman selling apples. Another, a pirate with a peg leg. He even appeared as Siamese twins. Now *that* was incredible!"

Mrs. Peacock, Miss Scarlet, and Professor Plum had been playing pinochle at a corner game table. The three of them looked up at once. "Let's see what's in the trunk!" Miss Scarlet said, laying down her cards.

Mr. Boddy scratched his head. "I'd love to open it but, as you can see, there are four locks and I don't have a key."

Quick as a wink, Professor Plum pulled a small cloth case out of his coat pocket, which he presented to Mr. Boddy. "Try these."

Mr. Boddy opened the case to find several unusual metal tools. "What are they?"

"Lock picks," replied Professor Plum.

"Forgive my rudeness for asking," Mrs. Peacock said, leaning forward in her seat, "but aren't they what burglars use? Why would you need them?"

"I'm always locking myself out of my lab or car," Plum explained sheepishly. "I got tired of calling a locksmith."

"But do they work?" Mr. Boddy wondered.

"Absolutely. If these can't open the locks, then they're not worth opening," replied Plum. "These picks are endorsed by S.T.E.A.L."

"What's that?" asked Colonel Mustard.

"The Society of Thieves, Embezzlers, And Lock-pickers."

Mr. Boddy promptly set to work on the locks.

Five minutes later . . .

Five minutes later the trunk was open, and everyone in the Billiard Room was coughing.

"Dust!" Mr. Boddy choked. "Years of dust and mildew!"

When the cloud of dust settled, the guests began to sift through the trunk, which was filled to the brim with magnificent costumes. Delicately embroidered vests. Elaborate animal masks. Full military uniforms with gold-braided epaulets and Napoleonic hats.

"I'm a whiz at detecting a disguise," bragged Mrs. White, who had joined the group in sorting through the trunk. "Put me in a room full of people in costume and I can guess their correct identity every time!"

"The same with me," said Miss Scarlet, wrapping a large red boa around her shoulders. "I'm never fooled. Not even at Halloween parties."

"It's not polite to brag," said Mrs. Peacock, coyly holding a fan in front of her face, "but I also have the ability to see through any masquerade."

"I find that hard to believe," scoffed Mr. Green, who had donned a World War II army helmet.

"Yes," added Professor Plum from behind a clown mask complete with red nose and bright-orange fright wig. "I think you'd have a tough time seeing through one of my disguises."

"We can prove it," declared Miss Scarlet.

"Is that a challenge?" asked Colonel Mustard, who was always up for a duel. To prove it, he flourished a large plastic sabre in the air several times, nearly knocking off Mr. Green's helmet.

The three women nodded firmly. "It's a challenge."

"Then we accept," said Mr. Green. "We men will disguise ourselves and see if you ladies can guess who we are."

"You're on!" cried Mrs. White, who was now

29

wearing a pair of Groucho Marx glasses with a large nose and mustache.

"Quite frankly, it'll be no contest," Miss Scarlet scoffed.

"What are we waiting for!" cried Mrs. Peacock. She put the fan back in the trunk and quickly donned a policeman's cap and whistle, which she blew. "Let's begin."

"Why don't the ladies adjourn to the Lounge for a cup of tea?" Mr. Boddy suggested. "I'll stay here and help the men with their disguises. We'll call you when we're ready."

The ladies hastened off to the Lounge, chattering happily among themselves. Meanwhile Green, Mustard, and Plum ransacked the trunk, trying on various items and striking silly poses for each other. Mr. Boddy watched approvingly.

"Good old Uncle N.E. Boddy," the host chuckled. "Even when he's not around, people are having fun."


Fifteen minutes later . . .


Fifteen minutes later, Mr. Boddy called the women back into the Billiard Room.

Mr. Boddy had dressed himself up like a magician in a black satin cape with red lining, white gloves, and black top hat. He gestured for the women to enter. "Feast your eyes and be amazed."

30

Mrs. White, Miss Scarlet, and Mrs. Peacock gasped in unison. "Oh, my!"

Before them stood three completely unrecognizable creatures: one in a full-body gorilla suit with a very realistic rubber mask; a clown in full makeup, baggy pants, and wig; and a knight in shining armor, his helmet visor tightly shut.

Mr. Boddy arranged the costumed guests in a line, then turned to face the women. "Anyone look familiar?"

"I recognize them all," said Miss Scarlet cockily. She flipped one end of the red boa she was still wearing over her shoulder, and pranced down the line, pointing at each man as she spoke. "The knight is Mr. Green, the clown is Colonel Mustard, and Plum is that ridiculous gorilla."

There was a long pause, as the three disguised men exchanged glances. Then Mr. Boddy flashed a mischievous grin. "Wrong on all counts!"

"What?" Miss Scarlet's face had turned the color of her boa. "Well, I never!" With that, she turned on her heel and marched over to the billiard table, where she sulked for the rest of the game.

"Anyone else care to hazard a guess?" Boddy asked, holding his gloved hands out to Mrs. Peacock and Mrs. White, who were both frowning with concentration.

Finally Mrs. Peacock turned to Mrs. White. "Why don't you go first, my dear?"

"No, after you," Mrs. White replied, taking a step backward.

"No, no, no, after you," Mrs. Peacock insisted, backing up, too.

"Age before beauty," Mrs. White said between clenched teeth.

Mrs. Peacock's eyes widened to two huge circles. "How rude!"

Hearing the women argue, the knight leaned over to the man beside him and whispered, "We fooled them, Colonel."

"Hush!" growled the other. "Now you've given us away."

Mrs. White, who had been snarling at Mrs. Peacock, suddenly raised her hand and began jumping up and down. "I know! I know! I know who's who!"

Mrs. Peacock put both hands on her hips. "How could you know," she demanded, "when Miss Scarlet and I don't?"

"Because I'm clever," Mrs. White retorted. She blew on her fingernails and polished them cockily on her uniform. "Using Miss Scarlet's wrong guess, and what I just overheard, I was able to figure it out — like that."

She snapped her fingers in triumph.

WHO ARE THE GUYS IN DISGUISE?

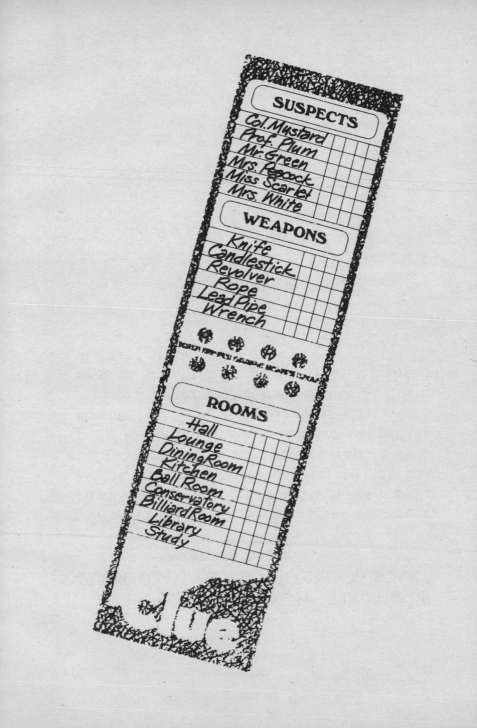

# SOLUTION

MR. GREEN is the clown, PROFESSOR PLUM is the knight, and COLONEL MUSTARD is wearing the gorilla suit.

We know that Miss Scarlet's guess was wrong on all counts. Therefore, Mr. Green was not the knight, Mustard was not the clown, and Plum was not the gorilla. Since the man in the armor whispered to Colonel Mustard, Mustard was not the knight. Therefore, Plum was the knight.

Since Mustard was not the knight or the clown, he must have been the gorilla. Which left Green disguised as the clown.

# 4.
# Your Chocolate or Your Life

"Gather around," Mr. Boddy said to his guests as they finished dinner one evening. "I have a delectable surprise for you, something I picked up on my recent trip to Switzerland."

With a dramatic flourish he presented a lavishly wrapped box covered in silver-and-gold paper and bound with a large red ribbon, which he set on the Dining Room table.

"How lovely," Miss Scarlet purred. "Is it a little something for me?"

"For all of you," Boddy replied, lifting the lid to expose a tray of delicate morsels coddled in cups of tissue paper. "These are the finest Swiss chocolates money can buy."

"I'd rather have a Swiss bank account," said Mr. Green.

"I'm awfully fond of Swiss steak," remarked Professor Plum.

"I think it's so sweet of you," Miss Scarlet trilled, waving a red-gloved hand.

"Too sweet, no doubt," murmured Mrs. Peacock, who was secretly on a diet.

"I'm nuts about sweets," added Colonel Mustard, reaching into the box.

"Just a moment," said Mr. Boddy, smoothly moving the box out of the Colonel's reach. "These chocolates are more than just tasty. In one of them is hidden the famous Gstaad Diamond."

"The Gstaad Diamond!" Mr. Green gasped. "You mean the diamond that skier found while leaving the chairlift on the Big Rock Candy Mountain?"

"The exact same diamond," Mr. Boddy replied. "I was given it as a gift just this past week. And now I'd like to give it to one of you."

Mr. Green whistled low. "Why, it must be worth millions."

Mr. Boddy just smiled in response.

"Which is the chocolate that has this diamond?" Miss Scarlet asked, seizing hold of the box. "I want to find it."

"Give that to me!" Mr. Green shouted, pulling the box away from her. "I'll find it if it's the last thing I do."

"It *will* be the last thing you do, if I have anything to say about it," barked Colonel Mustard as he muscled his way into the group struggling over the box.

"Ladies and gentlemen, please!" sputtered Mr. Boddy as he tried desperately to hang onto his precious box of chocolates. "Let's be civilized."

With a tremendous effort, he yanked the candy box out of their reach.

"Now let's handle this fairly and squarely," Mr. Boddy said. "I will allow each of you to pick one piece of chocolate." He raised a finger in warning. "But I will have no more fighting."

Just then the telephone rang. Mrs. White answered it.

"It's for you," she told Mr. Boddy. "It's some Swiss miss."

"Ah, that would be Ms. Zurich, my banker," Mr. Boddy replied. "She's in charge of my accounts in Switzerland. I'll take the call in my private office."

Mr. Boddy placed the box of chocolates in Mrs. White's arms with these instructions: "Make sure each guest receives only *one* piece."

"Yes, sir."

No sooner had Mr. Boddy left the room than all five guests lunged at Mrs. White. Quick as a wink she pulled a Revolver out of her apron.

"Stand back," she warned, "or I'll shoot. Now, kindly take your lumps. Of chocolate, I mean."

Miss Scarlet snatched up the biggest piece, certain that it contained the diamond. She checked to make sure her Lead Pipe was securely in her purse, then hurried off to a corner to inspect her chocolate. "This better have the Gstaad," she muttered darkly, "or someone will have to pay."

Mr. Green chose next and bit into his before he'd even removed the wrapper. "Dash it all," he grumbled. "I got a lousy caramel. I *hate* caramels." He left the room in a sulk.

Not wishing to chip a tooth, Colonel Mustard gave his choice a quick squeeze with his fingers. "Blast! Nothing." The old soldier forlornly shoved the remains of the mocha cream into his mouth. Then he took the lighted Candlestick from the Dining Room table and left.

Professor Plum made his selection next and dropped his chocolate into his pocket. "My bedtime snack," he announced as he left the room. "Sweet dreams."

Oblivious to the others, Mrs. Peacock was carefully slicing her choice in half with the knife. "One little taste will not ruin my diet plan." She took a tiny bite of her chocolate — only to find it filled with nuts. "I loathe nuts," she declared, and marched out of the room.

The only people left in the room were Mrs. White and Miss Scarlet. "I just can't decide," Mrs. White mumbled, running her fingers lightly over the tops of the chocolates. Finally she settled on a heart-shaped piece and carefully unwrapped it. The crisp crackling of the paper was so noisy that Mrs. White didn't notice Miss Scarlet sneaking up behind her.

*BONK!*

With a groan Mrs. White sank to the floor, still

clutching her weapon. Holding the Lead Pipe, Miss Scarlet stepped over the maid's prone body. She quickly took a bite from each of the remaining chocolates but the diamond was not in any of them.

"This is an outrage!" she spluttered. "I can't believe it, I . . . I feel *awful*." Miss Scarlet clutched her stomach and her face turned a sickening shade of green. "Too much chocolate," she gasped, slumping unconscious to the floor beside Mrs. White.

Just then Mr. Green tiptoed back into the room, the Rope dangling from his hand. "They're gone," he said aloud. "Now's my chance to bag the Gstaad. Ow!" He tripped over the bodies on the floor. "Mrs. White? Miss Scarlet? What happened?" Then he saw the ravaged box of chocolates. "Serves you right, the both of you," he sneered.

Mr. Green was so busy sneering, he didn't hear someone else enter the room. He turned just in time to be hit square on the head with the Candlestick.

*Thunk!*

The blow dropped Mr. Green to the floor with Mrs. White and Miss Scarlet.

The person who hit him started to search the pockets of the unconscious guests but, hearing the noise of feet coming down the corridor outside, hid next to the china cabinet.

Suddenly a man burst into the Dining Room.

"I've got it," he shouted. "I've got the diamond!

"Good heavens," he cried, seeing the three bodies on the floor. He knelt beside Mrs. White and patted one of her hands.

"Mrs. White, are you all right?"

A woman tiptoed ever so quietly into the room, with the Knife raised high above her head. She was about to stab the guest kneeling by the three bodies when she spied the shadow of the figure hiding beside the china cabinet. Throwing caution to the wind she rushed forward and stabbed at him.

She missed completely.

But her thrust had caused the man to lunge sideways. He ran smack dab into the wall.

*Thud!*

"My nose! It's bleeding," he cried in horror. "I can't stand the sight of blood!" The man wobbled for a moment, then fell backward in a faint, dropping his weapon.

The woman snatched his weapon from the floor, intending to use it on the gentleman with the diamond, who was still trying to revive the fallen Mrs. White.

"It's mine," the woman cried as she rushed toward the kneeling guest. "The diamond's all mine!"

But one of the victims on the floor suddenly regained consciousness and, raising up on one elbow, shot the woman and the man.

40

Grabbing the diamond, the murderer ran off, leaving Mr. Boddy to discover the crime.

## WHO COMMITTED THE DOUBLE MURDER AND STOLE THE DIAMOND?

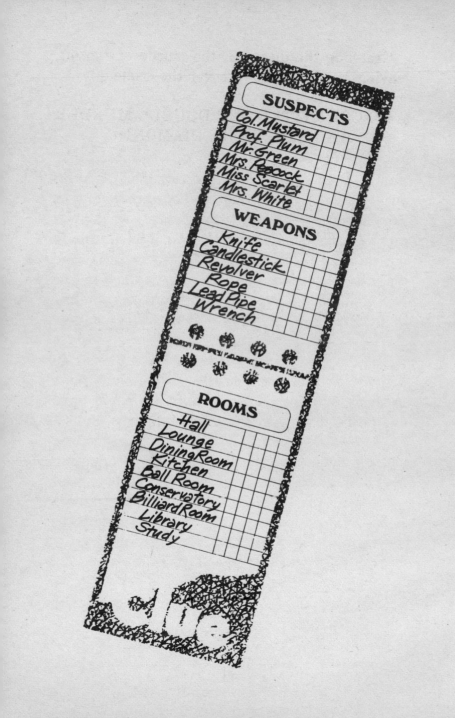

# SOLUTION

## MRS. WHITE killed PEACOCK and PLUM with the REVOLVER.

We know that Scarlet injured White and then fell sick on the floor. Then Green was hit by someone with a Candlestick, which we know to be Mustard from earlier in the story. Then a woman came in and stabbed at Mustard. That woman had to be Peacock since she was the only remaining woman. Mustard then bumped his nose on the wall, got a nosebleed, and passed out. Peacock and Plum were left standing, and both were killed by someone on the floor. That someone was Mrs. White, who had the Revolver.

Luckily for Peacock and Plum, Mrs. White, still stunned by the blow from the Lead Pipe, was seeing double when she fired the Revolver. Plus, her vision was so blurry she couldn't have hit the broadside of a barn. She not only missed Plum and Peacock, she missed grabbing the diamond as well. She grabbed the false double image of the diamond, and ran off with nothing more than a fistful of air.

# 5.
# Something Fishy

"Please pass the fish," Mr. Green said to the guests at lunch.

"But it's *all* fish," Mrs. Peacock replied, gesturing to the huge table laden with seafood. The menu included salmon jelly salad, cracked crab boats, clam chowder surprise, and sweet orange shrimp.

"Shrimp?" Mrs. White asked the guests with a smile. She passed the platter and they all grabbed for it at once. Seconds later she returned to the Kitchen with a completely empty plate. "Sharks," she mumbled as she pushed through the swinging doors.

"Does anyone notice anything fishy about this lunch?" asked Professor Plum as he stared at his plate. It appeared he had only just noticed that the luncheon included nothing but seafood.

"That's a deep question," said Mr. Boddy. "Let's dive into it."

"I could speak oceans about it," said Colonel Mustard.

"But then it would be so watered down," countered Miss Scarlet.

"Let's not argue," finished Mrs. Peacock. "We were all getting along so swimmingly."

As the laughter died down, Mr. Boddy chose that moment to make his announcement. He picked up his knife and gently tapped it against his water glass. "I suppose you're all wondering why I called you here today."

Colonel Mustard turned to Mr. Green and shrugged. "No. We always spend the weekend here."

"I know that," Mr. Boddy said. "But perhaps you're wondering why the entire luncheon fare is seafood."

This time Professor Plum replied. "Well, yes. I was indeed wondering why we were eating all of this fish."

"It's in celebration of my latest acquisition. It's really too thrilling." Mr. Boddy took a drink of water to calm himself. "You see, two days ago I purchased a Quazi-Motoh miniature grouper at the world-famous Bristy's auction house in the city."

"You bought a fish at an auction?" Mr. Green blinked in disbelief.

"Oh, yes. But not just any fish. There are only five like him in the entire world." Mr. Boddy beamed at his guests. "In fact, he is so rare, he's worth a million dollars."

"I'd clam up about that," whispered Mrs. White, who had just reentered with the coffee. "That's a lot of money to shell out."

At the mention of a million dollars, every guest's eyes lit up, and Mrs. White grinned wickedly.

"I'd like to see this fish," Miss Scarlet said, dabbing at her lips with a napkin as she pushed back her chair.

"Of course," Mr. Boddy replied. "That's why we're here."

He led the guests into the Study, where a small glass bowl was perched on a marble pedestal.

"Here he is, folks," Mr. Boddy said proudly. "Meet Clarence."

Clarence, a tiny rainbow-hued specimen, blinked out at the crowd of people surrounding his bowl.

"Poor fellow," Professor Plum murmured. "To have to spend his life in such a tiny bowl."

This gave Mr. Boddy a good chuckle. "The bowl's only temporary, Plum. I'm having a huge floor-to-ceiling aquarium built for Clarence. When it's finished, he'll have a home fit for a rare Quazi-Motoh."

Mrs. Peacock leaned down close to the bowl until she was eyeball-to-eyeball with Clarence. "He's so tiny. Why, he could almost fit in the palm of your hand."

"Or your purse," Miss Scarlet mused.

*Or a soup bowl*, Colonel Mustard thought.

"Or a tiny jam jar," Mrs. White added.

The guests adjourned to the Conservatory for coffee, each wrapped in their own thoughts about Clarence — the million-dollar fish.

One hour later . . .

One hour later, Mr. Green, toting a Revolver, returned quietly to the Study and scooped Clarence into his coffee cup, which he had filled with water. He started to leave, already counting the ways he would spend his million when he sold the fish.

Miss Scarlet, who had been spying on Mr. Green, lay in wait outside the Study door. She had stretched the Rope across the doorsill and pulled it taut as he drew closer.

Her trap worked perfectly. The unsuspecting Mr. Green tripped over the Rope, tossing the coffee cup and Clarence high in the air.

"Gotcha!" Miss Scarlet whispered as she caught Clarence and the still-full coffee cup.

Mr. Green wasn't so fortunate. His head hit the walnut paneling in the Hall and he was knocked out cold.

Miss Scarlet could hardly contain her joy as she headed for the grand staircase in the Hall. She planned to hurry to her room, pack, and then take Clarence on the shopping spree of a lifetime.

47

Her plans were cut short by a sharp jab in the ribs.

"Not so fast," a woman's voice rasped behind her. "I've been watching, and I think you have my coffee cup. Hand it over and don't turn around."

Miss Scarlet carefully passed the cup over her shoulder to the person with the Knife.

"Now run along," the person urged. "Go upstairs to your room, and don't look back."

Miss Scarlet did as she was told.

The guest with the Knife (and now Clarence) peered into the cup. "Why, you *are* tiny. Such a little thing to be worth *so* much money. Now hold on to your hat — I mean, fins. I'm taking you for a little ride."

Before the guest with the Knife could take even one step toward the front door, a masked man blocked the way. He had his hand in his coat pocket, holding what looked like a gun.

"I'll shoot," he bluffed, "unless you give me that coffee cup. There are only two like it, and they belong to Plum and me. Plum has his, so this one must be mine."

The guest with the Knife handed over the coffee cup and fled.

"All right, Clarence," the masked man chuckled. "It's time we cash in." He removed the Candlestick from his pocket and casually dropped it behind a potted plant.

Suddenly Mrs. Peacock appeared in the doorway to the Lounge. "There you are," she called pleasantly. "I've been looking all over for you."

The guest quickly removed his mask, so Mrs. Peacock wouldn't think anything odd. "What did you want me for?" the now unmasked man asked.

"I'm in charge of the coffee," Mrs. Peacock explained. "And it's time for me to pour you a fresh cup. Yours must be ice-cold by now."

"Um . . . er . . . uhh . . ." The unmasked man was caught completely off guard. Not able to think of a quick escape, he allowed Mrs. Peacock to lead him into the Lounge.

"Good afternoon," another guest called from the wing-backed chair. "I've just been catching up on the day's news and enjoying a lovely cup of coffee. Isn't it delicious? Mocha java guava, I think."

"Yes, well, I must be going." The man broke free of Mrs. Peacock's grasp and bolted for the nearest exit. Before he could reach the door, Mrs. Peacock hurled a huge iron Wrench at him. It caught him square on the back of the head, knocking him out.

Once again the coffee cup, with Clarence inside, flew through the air. It fell to the ground and exploded into hundreds of little pieces.

Clarence, now a fish out of water, flopped helplessly on the Lounge floor.

Mrs. Peacock made a dive to rescue the fish but before she could scoop him up, the guest in the chair took a weapon out of his coat and swung at the tiny, wiggling creature.

*WHAP!*

"There, I've killed that old cockroach," the guest in the chair said. "Imagine, hiding in people's coffee cups. Dreadful!"

## WHO KILLED CLARENCE?

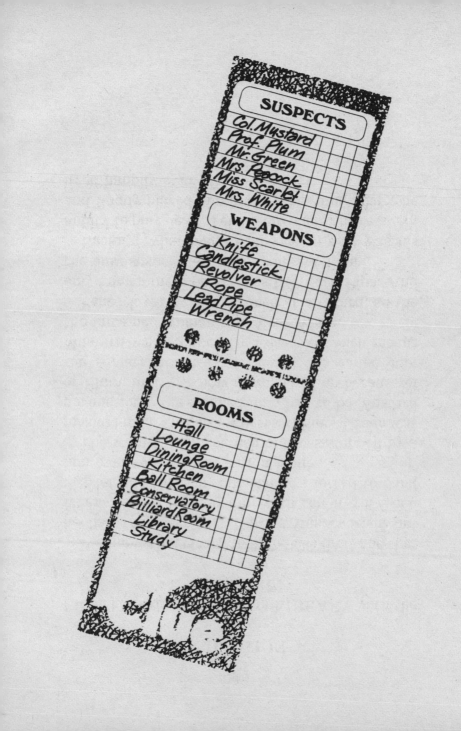

# SOLUTION

## PROFESSOR PLUM in the LIBRARY with the LEAD PIPE

We know that Green took the fish first, and that he had the Revolver. But he was knocked out when Scarlet tripped him with the Rope. Then Scarlet had the fish, but she was forced to hand him over to a woman with a Knife.

The woman took the fish but was stopped by a masked man with a Candlestick. Since Green was unconscious, the masked man had to be Mustard or Plum, and we know it wasn't Plum because of the remark about Plum having his coffee cup. Mustard was stopped by Peacock, which means the unnamed woman was Mrs. White.

Peacock threw the Wrench at Mustard, so the only remaining weapon was the Lead Pipe. And the only suspect left was Professor Plum.

Luckily, what made Clarence so rare was his ability to play dead. Ten minutes later he revived, and Boddy placed him in the aquarium, where he lived happily ever after.

# 6.
# Who Bent the Bentley?

"**W**hat a perfect day for a drive in the country," Miss Scarlet purred to Mr. Boddy. The guests had gathered in the Study to make plans for the weekend. "Couldn't you take us for a tiny spin in one of your beautiful cars?"

"Sorry, I can't," Mr. Boddy said, checking his watch. "I'm waiting to hear from my broker. However, I do have an entire fleet of cars at your disposal."

"A whole fleet?" repeated Mrs. Peacock.

"Yes, you may take any car in the garage you like," Mr. Boddy said, slipping into the big leather chair behind his desk. "Except the Bentley."

"But why can't we take the Bentley?" demanded Colonel Mustard, who now wanted to drive it more than any other car.

"Yes, why can't we take the Bentley?" Mr. Green leaned over the desk. "Don't you trust us?"

"You can trust me, I'm an excellent driver," Professor Plum boasted. "I've never hit a soul. All of those accidents were the other drivers' faults."

"It's not that I don't trust you," explained Mr. Boddy. "It's just that the Bentley is one of my most prized possessions. It's so valuable that even *I* don't drive it. It's more of an investment, really." Mr. Boddy held his arms open to the group. "Surely, you can all understand that?"

The guests understood, but they didn't like it. Not one of them moved. They just stood in a line in front of the desk, staring sullenly at their host.

*Brrrring!*

"There's my call. Bye-bye now." Mr. Boddy waved them away cheerily. "Mrs. White will show you to the garage. Have a good time, all of you."

One by one they shuffled out of the room, grumbling to themselves and each other.

"Unfair," the man in the yellow blazer declared. "Simply unfair, by Jove."

The woman in red agreed with him. "Why, he's just an old party pooper."


Ten minutes later . . .


Ten minutes later, the guests had changed into their driving clothes and were standing outside the vast garage where Mr. Boddy stored his fleet of vintage cars.

Colonel Mustard, now dressed in a yellow canvas coat and driving goggles, suggested they take the yellow Rolls-Royce. "It's not the Bentley, but for my money, it's the next best thing."

"Never settle for second best." Mr. Green ran one green-gloved hand along the door of a sleek emerald sports car. "The Ferrari is the one for us."

"Don't be ridiculous," huffed Mrs. Peacock, who had donned deep-blue gloves, goggles, and a floor-length driving coat with a blue hood. "That car is too tiny to fit us all. I say we take the sky-blue Edsel. It's so roomy."

"Well, if it's room you want, madam," Professor Plum replied, "the purple Packard fits the bill." He patted the hood of the massive vehicle, which boomed a resonant echo in reply. "Big and beautiful."

Miss Scarlet didn't speak. Dressed in sleek red leather pants and vest, she stared awestruck at the gleaming red Bentley with its plush leather interior.

"It's simply magnificent," she whispered to the others. "Oh, please! Let's take it for a spin. Mr. Boddy will never know."

Mrs. White, who had washed and polished the car for two years without ever being allowed to drive it, declared, "That's a brilliant idea. But on one condition — I get to drive."

The others opened their mouths in protest, but she held up a solid-gold car key and chain. "Ah, ah, ah. Remember, I have the key."

"Oh, all right," Miss Scarlet said, her ruby-red lips forming a pout. "You go ahead and drive. At least I'll get to ride in it."

Mr. Green took an impromptu vote. "All in favor of taking the Bentley, say aye."

"Aye!" five voices chorused.

Mr. Green turned to the lone dissenter, the woman in blue, and gave her his most menacing glare. "Opposed?"

"You all are too rude," huffed Mrs. Peacock, her voice quivering with indignation. "Stealing Mr. Boddy's prize vehicle when he specifically asked you not to touch it."

"What do you intend to do about it?" challenged Miss Scarlet.

"I'm telling," replied Mrs. Peacock. Her blue eyes twinkled as thoughts of the great reward she'd receive from Mr. Boddy for saving his beloved Bentley danced in her head. But before she could take a single step toward the door, a deep voice barked, "Get her!"

Four angry guests surrounded her, assisted by Mrs. White, who helped bind Mrs. Peacock's hands together with the Rope. Miss Scarlet tied a red chiffon scarf around Mrs. Peacock's mouth, and the five of them ushered her to the Edsel.

"Ooh, you were right," Miss Scarlet said as they bundled Mrs. Peacock into the backseat and locked the door. "It *is* roomy."

Professor Plum turned on the car radio, and

then shouted through the open window vent. "Don't worry, Mrs. Peacock, we'll be back in a few hours. In the meantime sit back and enjoy the music."

"Now!" Mrs. White said, twirling the gold key with a dramatic flourish. "On to the Bentley!"

She opened the door and slipped behind the wheel. Mr. Green opened the door on the other side and slid into the passenger seat beside her.

"I positively must have a window seat," Colonel Mustard declared, staking his claim in the back.

"So must I," Professor Plum said. "Otherwise I have a tendency to get carsick."

Miss Scarlet wrinkled her nose, saying, "Oh, all right. I'll sit in the middle." However, she made sure to step on Mustard's foot with the stiletto heel of her red shoe as she climbed over him to get to her place.

Mrs. White started the engine and eased the car out of the garage and down the long drive that led to the Boddy mansion. They held their breaths as they passed the Study window, then breathed a collective sigh of relief at the sight of Mr. Boddy's head bent in concentration over his desk.

"Phew!"

Mrs. White stepped on the gas, and the luxurious car zoomed out of the gate onto the highway. The passengers leaned back in their seats, ready to enjoy the drive.

The Bentley hadn't traveled more than a mile before the engine began to sputter and cough.

"Good heavens!" Colonel Mustard clutched the seat in front of him as the car lurched forward. "This isn't a very smooth ride. What in blazes is the matter?"

The car jerked once more, and then wheezed to a halt.

Mrs. White glanced down at the dashboard and gasped in astonishment, "We're out of gas!"

"That's ridiculous," Miss Scarlet said, rolling her eyes in frustration. "We just passed a gas station a half mile back. Why didn't you stop there?"

"I forgot to check the gauge, okay?" Mrs. White snapped back. "Any one of you could have looked." She turned on Mr. Green in exasperation. "Why didn't you notice we were out of fuel?"

"Don't look at me. I'm just a passenger," Mr. Green replied. "It's up to the driver to watch out for that sort of thing."

"Obviously we need a new driver," Professor Plum remarked.

"That's what I said in the first place," Miss Scarlet agreed. "This wouldn't have happened if *I'd* been behind the wheel."

"You drive? Over my dead body," Mrs. White retorted.

"That can be easily arranged," Miss Scarlet said with a smile.

"Stop this bickering at once!" Colonel Mustard barked. "That's an order!" When the others were quiet, he continued in his best military manner. "Our plan of action is simple — we'll just hike back for gas. Green, you come with me. Plum — you wait here with the ladies."

Half an hour later . . .

Half an hour later, the Colonel and Mr. Green returned, covered with dust from the road, and carrying the emergency gas can. The sun was now at high noon and both men were pouring sweat. They collapsed in the shade by the side of the road while Plum filled the tank. When it was time to leave, Green made a dive for the driver's side of the car.

"I'm doing the driving this time," he insisted.

"Why you and not me?" Mrs. White asked.

"Because," Mr. Green explained, "I hiked all the way back to the gas station, and carried the extremely heavy can all the way back to the Bentley."

"I say," Colonel Mustard protested, "so did I."

"But *I* paid for it," Mr. Green said smugly.

Reluctantly, Mrs. White surrendered the keys to Mr. Green and they all piled back in the car. Mr. Green took the wheel and off they went down the beautiful tree-lined road. Unfortunately, they didn't go far, because Mr. Green, who was leading the group in a rousing chorus of "Greensleeves," didn't notice the box of nails in the center of the road and ran right over it.

*Blam!*

The explosion sounded like cannon fire and the car careened all over the road as Green tried to regain control of it.

"We're under attack!" Colonel Mustard bellowed. "Hit the dirt."

"Don't be an idiot!" Miss Scarlet shouted back at him. "We've had a blowout. The tire is flat."

Mustard, who had thrown himself to the floor of the car, raised up angrily. "Nobody calls me an idiot and lives to tell about it."

But before Mustard could draw his Revolver to challenge Miss Scarlet to a duel, Mr. Green had pulled to the side of the road and hit the brakes. The guests and Mrs. White were thrown forward against the dashboard or the seat in front of them.

"You've already flattened the tire," Mrs. White complained, rubbing her nose gingerly. "You don't have to flatten us, too."

Mr. Green just folded his arms and sulked. "I don't care if it was my fault. I'm not changing the tire. It's somebody else's turn."

Colonel Mustard was still smarting from Miss Scarlet's harsh words as well as the sharp bonk he'd received on the nose when the car screeched to a halt. He turned to face the ladies and declared, "Green's right. I think Miss Scarlet and Mrs. White should change the tire."

"That's ridiculous! Look at these nails," Miss Scarlet gasped, holding out her elegant fingers. "I just had a manicure."

"I don't do tires," declared Mrs. White. "I also don't do windows."

"Well, you'd better do *this*," Colonel Mustard shot back, "or else we don't go anywhere."

Mrs. White turned to Professor Plum as they all got out of the Bentley. "You're going to help us," she said flatly. "All you did last time was pour the gasoline into the tank."

One hour later . . .

One hour later, five filthy folks got back into the Bentley.

"Oh no you don't!" Mrs. White grabbed the back of Mr. Green's coat as he headed for the driver's seat. "You're the one who got us into this mess."

Miss Scarlet grasped Mrs. White by the white collar of her maid's uniform. "You've already had your turn. Give me the keys."

"No!" Colonel Mustard bellowed, leaping between them. "Give them to me. I'm the leader here."

"Who elected you?" Professor Plum demanded.

A huge battle ensued. Suffice it to say that when the dust cleared and they were all back in the

Bentley, no one was sitting where they were before.

The driver made a U-turn and headed for home, anxious to be rid of the four grumpy passengers. But within seconds Colonel Mustard and the driver were arguing over which radio station to play.

"I like a good-spirited Oldies station," the Colonel announced, flipping the dial.

"I prefer Easy Listening," the driver replied, moving the dial back.

"Oldies!" Colonel Mustard spun the dial hard to the right.

"Easy Listening!" the driver cried and spun it back.

"Look out!" the three passengers in the backseat shouted.

But they were too late. The Bentley swerved off the road and ran smack into a massive oak tree. The crumpled hood popped up with a groan, while the punctured radiator spewed water and steam every which way.

No one was hurt but all were badly shaken. Finally one of the guests dialed Mr. Boddy on the car phone and said these four words: "We bent the Bentley."

Fifteen minutes later . . .

Fifteen minutes later, Mr. Boddy drove up in the purple Packard. Seated beside him in the front

62

seat was a very smug Mrs. Peacock. Mr. Boddy parked the Packard next to the Bentley, where everyone was standing looking dazed and a bit bruised.

"What on earth happened?" a distraught Mr. Boddy demanded. "And who bent my Bentley?"

No one could remember who was driving, or what had happened.

"I'm afraid I didn't see a thing," Professor Plum said, trying to straighten out his glasses, which had gotten crunched in the crash. "I had a window seat and was looking outside at the time of the accident."

"All I remember," Mustard moaned, rubbing the bruise on his forehead where he'd bashed against the radio dial, "is that I was sitting next to a woman."

Mrs. White scowled and said, "I was sitting beside Mr. Green, who refused to sit in the middle."

"Aha!" cried Boddy. "From what you just described, I now know who bent my Bentley."

## WHO WAS DRIVING THE BENTLEY?

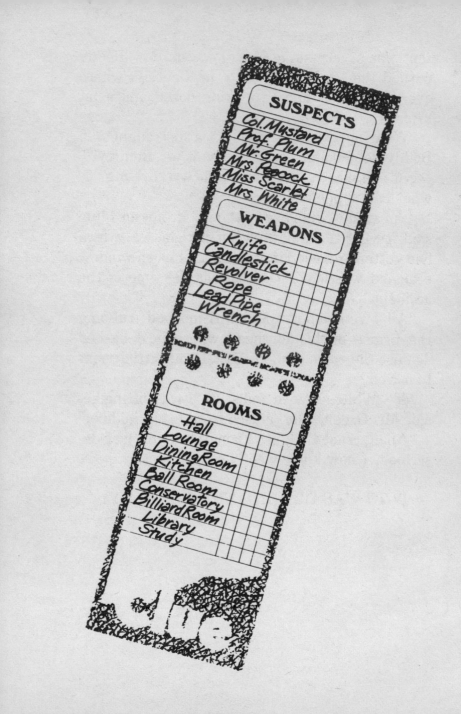

# SOLUTION

## MISS SCARLET

We know that Mrs. White drove first, and that she then changed places with Mr. Green after they ran out of gas. And we know that after the flat tire they all switched seats, with no one sitting where they'd sat before.

After the accident, Mustard was seated next to a woman.

Mrs. White remembered sitting beside Green, who refused to sit in the middle. This tells us he had a window seat in the back and that White was next to him. Plum also said he had a window seat.

We know that Mustard tried to adjust the radio, so he was in the front seat. And since he was sitting next to a woman, and Miss Scarlet was the only other woman, she must have been driving the Bentley.

# 7.
# The Slumber-less Party

"**B**rrr, it's cold in here!" complained Miss Scarlet.

A deep, heavy snow was falling outside the Conservatory window. She and the other guests had just finished another grand dinner with Mr. Boddy and had gathered there to say good night.

"Perhaps," noted Mrs. Peacock, "if you dressed a bit more warmly . . ." She gestured toward Miss Scarlet's sleeveless red satin gown. "Things wouldn't be so chilled. I always wear a muffler myself."

Mrs. Peacock flashed the tag of her famous Dee Zyner blue knitted muffler. She wore the muffler over a sweater-vest that she had buttoned to the very top button. The vest covered a turtleneck sweater, which covered two layers of long underwear.

"Yes, it is a bit cold. Mrs. White?" Mr. Boddy called to his maid. "Would you mind checking the furnace?"

"Not at all, sir," Mrs. White replied with a cheery smile. The moment she turned her back

66

the smile became a scowl. "No, I don't mind going into that dark, freezing basement with hundreds of little beady rodent eyes staring at me from every corner," she muttered as she left the room. "I don't mind at all."

While they waited for Mrs. White's return, the guests huddled together at the window.

"It's a regular winter wonderland out there," Professor Plum declared as he stared out the window at the thick curtain of falling snow.

"It's more like a transportation nightmare," Mr. Green countered. "With snow that heavy, cars won't start, roads won't be plowed, and all business transactions will screech to a halt."

Miss Scarlet shrugged. "If it were warm in here, you wouldn't feel that way. I'll bet you'd think it was all rather cozy."

"Not a chance," Mr. Green shot back. "Snow is not cozy. It's wet and messy."

Just then Mrs. White came back in. She was out of breath, having raced down the creaky basement stairs to the furnace, then back up to the light. She grasped a large Wrench in her hand, more for warding off mice than fixing the furnace.

"It's broken," Mrs. White panted, leaning against the doorsill. "I can't repair it myself, and the repairman can't reach the mansion due to the snow."

Miss Scarlet frowned. "You mean, we won't have any heat?"

"Not unless you know how to fix a furnace," Mrs. White said, offering the Wrench to Miss Scarlet.

"Don't be ridiculous." Miss Scarlet shooed the Wrench away from her with one elegant red-gloved hand. "Get that away from me."

"How inconvenient," Mr. Boddy said. He flipped on a light switch to test it, and the chandeliers blazed brightly. "At least the electricity still works."

"A lot of good that does us," Mr. Green groused. "A proper host would have insisted on electric heat as a backup."

Mrs. Peacock turned and stared balefully at Boddy. "I'd love to stay and freeze with you, but I really must be going. Back to my home. Where the furnace works."

Mr. Green and Professor Plum stepped forward. "We're leaving, too."

"Well, I suppose you have to do what you have to do," Mr. Boddy said with a sigh. "I'll see you to the door."

A crestfallen Mr. Boddy walked his guests to the front door in the Hall. But when he tried to open the door, it wouldn't budge. "I believe the door is blocked by a large snowdrift," Mr. Boddy declared. "This storm is worse than I thought. Quick, everyone, try the windows."

The guests, now grimly determined to get out

of the mansion, raced from the Conservatory to the Library to the Billiard Room to the Ball Room, trying to find one door or window that would open.

"It's no use," Colonel Mustard finally announced. "We're snowed in. We'll have to make camp here for the night."

"Camp!" Mr. Boddy cried. "What an excellent idea. We can have a slumber party."

Mrs. Peacock looked positively horrified at the idea.

"Don't worry," Mr. Boddy assured her. "I have plenty of camping gear. We can each pitch a tent in the Ballroom in front of the fireplace. It'll be just like camping out, without the nuisance of bugs or wild animals."

Professor Plum was the only one who found the camping out idea appealing. "Can we roast marshmallows?" he asked eagerly.

"We'll even tell stories around the campfire and sing songs," Boddy announced, clapping him on the back. "You'll see. It'll be loads of fun."

"Well, I for one am not sleeping in my clothes," Miss Scarlet declared. "I'll need to change into something more comfortable."

"What do you say we all change into our pj's," Mr. Boddy suggested, "then meet back here for the slumber party?"

"Not on your life," Mrs. Peacock said primly. "The clothes I'm wearing are just fine, thank you."

"Well, then, er, what do you say those who wish to change into their pj's do so, and meet back here in twenty minutes."

Professor Plum checked his pocket watch. "Perfect."

"Well, if we have to . . ." shrugged Mr. Green.

Mr. Boddy was so excited at the prospect of an indoor camp-out that he skipped out of the room. "See you shortly, then, fellow campers!"

As he left, Colonel Mustard turned to face the others. "You'd better not snore," he said grimly. "Any of you. That's the one thing I can't abide."

Twenty minutes later . . .

Twenty minutes later, the guests met back in the Ballroom. As none of them trusted the others to safely share the same sleeping quarters, each brought along a weapon. The fire in the massive hearth was blazing, and Mrs. White, with a Revolver tucked into her apron pocket, had prepared hot chocolate, and marshmallows for roasting.

"I have six tents," said Boddy, gesturing to the color-coded pup tents that had been erected around the Ball Room, "for your comfort and pleasure."

Mrs. White took the white tent. Green grabbed the green tent. Plum took the purple, and Peacock the blue. Mustard's was canary yellow and Miss Scarlet's a vibrant red. The guests unrolled their sleeping bags inside their tents and then, at Mr. Boddy's insistence, gathered around the fireplace for stories, songs, and marshmallows.

*Bong!*

The clock struck midnight just as Mr. Boddy was about to tell them the absolutely true story of the one-armed man whose hook got caught on top of a car not two miles from the Boddy mansion.

Mr. Green was the first to leap to his feet. "Well, I'm tired. Good night, all."

The others quickly followed his lead and settled into their tents.

Mr. Boddy waited until everyone was asleep, then tiptoed up to his bedroom where he watched television in cozy comfort, warmed by his private electric heater.

Hours later . . .

Hours later, Mrs. White became overheated from sleeping too close to the fire.

"Too hot!" she muttered, stumbling out of her tent and heading for Colonel Mustard's, which was the furthest from the fire. She woke him. The Colonel, still half asleep and clutching his Lead Pipe, agreed to switch tents with her.

Mrs. White was so sleepy that she forgot to bring her weapon to her new tent.

"Too cold!' Professor Plum mumbled only moments later. He left his tent and curled up as close

71

to the fire as possible. Cradled in his arms was the Candlestick.

"Too loud!" Miss Scarlet had been rudely awakened by Mrs. White, who was snoring loudly in the tent beside hers. She tucked her weapon into the pocket of her robe and took Professor Plum's tent. But first she tiptoed into Peacock's tent and stole the Wrench.

"Be quiet!" Miss Scarlet rasped, hurling the Wrench at Mrs. White's tent in an attempt to stop the snoring. It didn't.

"Too bright!" Mr. Green, clutching the handle of his weapon, sat bolt upright in his tent. The light from the Hall chandelier was shining directly on his face. He crawled out of his tent and, finding the red tent vacant, took that. Moments later he was sound asleep, snoring like a buzz saw.

"Too hard," the person in the yellow tent muttered. "I'm going upstairs to my bedroom. It may be cold but at least my back won't hurt."

The guest closest to the fire followed suit. "Soft bed. Give me a soft bed."

"Where are my plugs?" The person in the white tent felt in the pocket of his robe, and found a pair of "Noises Off" ear plugs. He slipped them into his ears and slept like a log till morning.

"Brrrrr!" Miss Scarlet said with a shiver. Realizing the fire had gone down and there were no more logs, she stole a muffler from one of the other guests and wrapped herself in it tightly. She replaced the muffler with her weapon, draping it around the unsuspecting guest's neck. Nice and warm at last, Miss Scarlet returned to sleep.

The guest Miss Scarlet had just visited suddenly sat up and turned in the direction of the horrendously loud snoring. "That noise! I can't take it anymore. I'm going to stop it once and for all."

Half an hour later . . .

Half an hour later, one of the snoring guests was discovered strangled.

WHO KILLED WHOM?

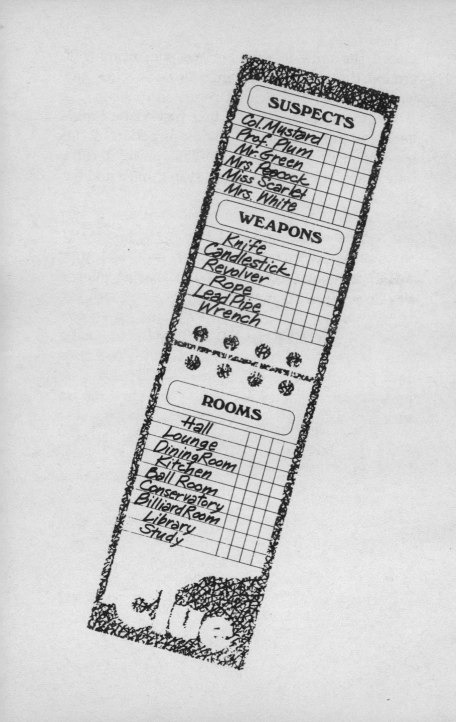

## SUSPECTS

Col. Mustard
Prof. Plum
Mr. Green
Mrs. Peacock
Miss Scarlet
Mrs. White

## WEAPONS

Knife
Candlestick
Revolver
Rope
Lead Pipe
Wrench

## ROOMS

Hall
Lounge
Dining Room
Kitchen
Ball Room
Conservatory
Billiard Room
Library
Study

# SOLUTION

## MRS. PEACOCK killed MR. GREEN with the ROPE in the BALL ROOM.

We know that only two people snore — Mrs. White and Mr. Green. But we know that White, having exchanged tents with Mustard, left the yellow tent and went upstairs. Therefore, Green must have been the victim.

With White and Plum (the guest by the fire) now upstairs, and Mustard snoozing away with his ear plugs on — only Scarlet and Peacock could be the suspects. But knowing that Miss Scarlet returned to sleep after leaving her weapon (the Rope) wrapped around Peacock's neck, we also know that only Mrs. Peacock was left to commit the murder.

Luckily, Mr. Green was not dead, but merely suffering from oxygen deprivation. He was revived by Miss Scarlet, who woke up because the Ball Room was — too quiet.

# 8.
# Foul Ball

*W*hack!

It was Mr. Boddy's turn in the game of croquet and he hit the ball soundly, sending it whizzing through two wickets.

Colonel Mustard patted him on the back. "Way to whack it!"

The other guests wandered through the lavish gardens, thoroughly enjoying the lovely spring afternoon.

Miss Scarlet, dressed in a rose-covered sundress and straw hat, smiled at Mrs. Peacock. "Have you noticed how well we're all getting along?"

"Yes, I have." Mrs. Peacock smiled back. "It's lovely, isn't it? No one has raised a voice, which I think is so rude — "

"Or raised a mallet," Professor Plum cut in pleasantly. "Which can be not only rude, but painful." Plum looked very dapper in his lavender knickers and matching sports coat. His bow tie was crooked and one purple argyle sock sagged, but that was par for the course.

"Yoo-hoo!" a voice trilled from the window of the mansion. Mrs. White stuck her head out the Library window. Even she seemed to have caught spring fever. She fluttered her cleaning rag at Mr. Boddy. "Phone call. It's your nephew, Bartholomew Benjamin Best-Boddy."

"A charming lad," Mr. Boddy said, setting his mallet against a wrought-iron garden bench. "But somewhat short — on cash, that is!"

Mr. Green, who considered himself an expert on money matters, cupped one hand over his mouth and whispered loudly, "You mean, the kid's broke?"

"Flat broke," Mr. Boddy replied. "Which really makes no difference to me. I'm so fond of little Bart that I had a statue of him sculpted in marble."

Mrs. Peacock, who had missed her wicket for the last three turns, was anxious to leave the game. "I just love sculpture," she gushed. "May I see it?"

"Of course. Come with me to the Conservatory." Mr. Boddy offered Mrs. Peacock his arm and the two of them strolled up to the mansion.

While Mrs. Peacock admired the marble statue that stood in a place of honor on the grand piano, Mr. Boddy picked up the phone.

"Hello, Bartholomew!" he said. "What a pleasant surprise!"

Before Mr. Boddy could proceed any further

with his conversation, a croquet ball smashed through the Conservatory window. It barely missed Mrs. Peacock before shattering the statue of Mr. Boddy's nephew into a thousand pieces.

"Oh, dear," Mr. Boddy said, blinking in surprise at the remains of the marble statue scattered across his carpet. "I'm afraid you've been broken."

"Yes, I *am* broke," replied his nephew. "It's the reason I'm calling, Uncle."

Mr. Boddy noticed that Mrs. Peacock, who ducked when the ball whizzed through the window, had not reappeared from behind the piano. On closer inspection, he discovered that she had completely passed out from shock.

"Look, Barty, I'm going to have to ring you back," Mr. Boddy said, fanning Mrs. Peacock's face. "We've had an — an unfortunate incident here. I'll explain later."

He hung up the phone and grabbed a vase of fresh-cut flowers sitting on the table near the piano. Pulling out the roses, he tossed the water in the vase onto Mrs. Peacock's face.

"Flood!" Mrs. Peacock gasped. "Everyone into the ark."

"I'm glad you're back with us, Mrs. Peacock," Mr. Boddy said as he handed her his monogrammed handkerchief. "Excuse me a moment, will you? I've got to check up on a foul ball."

Mr. Boddy hurried out of the Conservatory,

leaving a dazed and dripping Mrs. Peacock behind.

"One of you just broke the statue of Bartholomew Benjamin Best-Boddy," Boddy charged when he reached the croquet players. "Who did it?"

"It certainly wasn't me," said Mr. Green.

"It was Mrs. Peacock," Colonel Mustard barked, raising his mallet. "And I'll challenge her to a duel for you."

"No, it was Mr. Green." Miss Scarlet pointed her mallet at the guest in the green linen suit.

Professor Plum shook his head vehemently. "No, I'm sure it wasn't Mr. Green."

Mrs. White, who had been cleaning the windows of the Library and had witnessed the wayward whacking, shouted, "I saw the whole thing. And I know for a fact that only one of you is telling the truth. The rest of you are lying."

"Aha!" cried Mr. Boddy with glee. "Then I've figured out who smashed the statue of my bemusing and always broke nephew, Bartholomew Benjamin Best-Boddy."

## WHO BROKE THE STATUE?

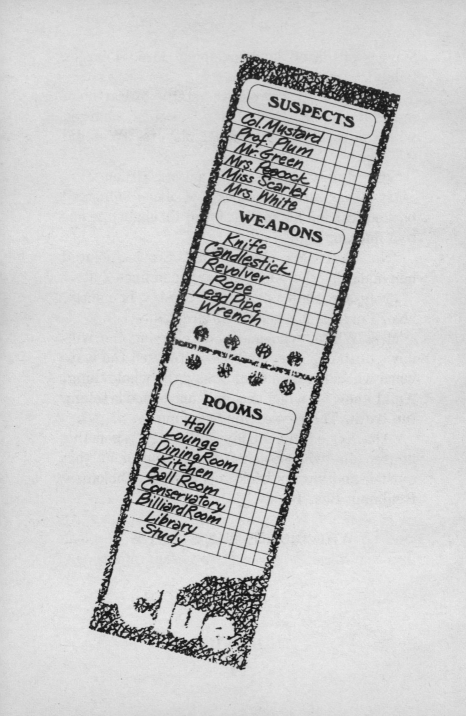

# 18

# SOLUTION

## MR. GREEN

Although Mrs. Peacock was accused, she was inside — and, as a result, innocent. Plum and Green both claimed that Green was innocent — yet our eyewitness, Mrs. White, said only *one* guest was telling the truth. So Plum and Green are lying. Therefore, Scarlet is the guest who is telling the truth.

Bad news for Bartholomew B-B-B. With the statue smashed, Boddy put his prodigal nephew out of mind for a time, and therefore, out of pocket change.

# 9.
# Time Is Running Out

On the morning of Friday the thirteenth, each of Mr. Boddy's favorite friends received the following letter:

> *Dear Friends,*
> *Though we've had many wonderful and surprise-filled times together, one or more of you always seems to arrive too early or too late, which puts a damper on the festivities. To entice you to pay more attention to time, I'm planning an extra special party tonight. It begins at the stroke of midnight. The one of you who arrives at my front door precisely on the hour will be handed a check for fifty thousand dollars by Mrs. White, who will be keeping the time. I know you won't want to miss this party.*
>
> > *Your loyal friend,*
> > *Mr. Boddy*

Miss Scarlet read her invitation carefully, then tucked it into her purse. She had every intention of winning that fifty thousand dollars.

As she selected her outfit for the evening — ruby-red satin gown, red spike-heel shoes, and ruby-encrusted watch — she methodically planned her schedule. "It'll take ten minutes to drive to Mr. Boddy's mansion. Of course I'll need to allow five minutes to freshen my makeup and five minutes to walk to the front door in these spike heels."

Across town, another guest was making her own preparations. Mrs. Peacock, upon receiving her invitation, had dashed to her closet in a panic. "Simply nothing to wear. I've got nothing at all to wear."

She flipped through the long row of dresses hanging in neat plastic bags on the rack. "Too short. Too tight. Too revealing. Too much."

Finally, when she was just about to give up on the party and the fifty thousand dollars, Mrs. Peacock discovered the perfect gown, hidden way in the back. It was a floor-length tent dress, made from a sturdy double-knit material that wouldn't *dream* of clinging to any part of the wearer's body.

"Just right," she sighed.

Mrs. Peacock checked the industrial-strength watch she wore on a thick black leather band on her wrist. "If I plan this right — first calling a cab and allowing fifteen minutes for it to arrive, then fifteen minutes to get to Mr. Boddy's front door, making sure, of course, that the driver pays strict attention to the speed limit — then I should arrive at midnight on the nose."

Colonel Mustard, who'd also received an invitation, hummed to himself as he planned the varied ways he would spend his fifty thousand. He had donned his favorite top hat with the yellow band and his yellow bow tie and was polishing his saddle and riding equipment in his stables.

"Of course, I'll ride my trusty steed, Sergeant, over to the Boddy mansion," he declared as he slapped the jet-black gelding good-naturedly on the right flank. "I'll need fifteen minutes to get there, ten minutes to stable Sergeant, and five minutes to cover the distance from the Boddy stables to the mansion's front door. If my calculations are correct — which of course they are — I should leave here precisely at twenty-three thirty hours. Operation Jackpot will be a snap."

Across town, Mr. Green slipped one arm into his green satin dinner jacket and paused to check his high-priced green watch, which was guaranteed to keep perfect time. He put the watch to his ear and smiled. "Purring like a precise, punctual cat." He slipped his arm into his other sleeve and went over his agenda once more. "Ten minutes to drive to the mansion, five minutes to set my expensive, extensive car alarm, and five more to get to the door. That money's in the bank — *my* bank."

"Oh my," Professor Plum mumbled pleasantly. "This does look nice." He was standing in front of his own full-length mirror, admiring his reflection. Plum had donned his purple academic gown with the many ribbons that went with his numerous (mostly honorary) degrees. It was his favorite costume for formal occasions.

"Yes, this is just the outfit a person should wear when receiving fifty thousand dollars." He carefully placed his purple mortarboard hat on top of his head, and smiled at himself. "It's a lovely night for a walk. I'll give myself exactly thirty minutes to walk from here to Mr. Boddy's front door. Yes, thirty minutes should just do it."

Their preparations complete, each guest spent the rest of the evening daydreaming about the fifty thousand dollars he or she would win at the stroke of midnight.

At eleven-thirty P.M. . . .

At eleven-thirty P.M.:
Colonel Mustard and Sergeant trotted up the road toward the Boddy mansion.

Mrs. Peacock phoned for a cab.

Professor Plum, looking very regal in his purple robe, headed down the road toward the mansion on foot.

Ten minutes later:

Mr. Green pulled out of his driveway.

85

Miss Scarlet put the pedal to the metal of her red Ferrari.

Unfortunately . . .

Unfortunately, Mrs. Peacock's cab broke all speed records on the highway, screeching to a halt in front of Mr. Boddy's front door ten minutes sooner than she had anticipated.

The cab's reckless ride down the highway frightened Sergeant the horse, who broke into a gallop, putting the Colonel five minutes ahead of schedule.

Professor Plum, quite the academic sight, attracted the attention of a former student, who offered to give him a lift to the Boddy mansion just five minutes away. Plum accepted the ride, completely forgetting that he had only been walking for twenty minutes, and he had allowed himself a full thirty minutes to walk to the mansion.

Miss Scarlet arrived exactly as planned, nearly running over an extremely irate Mrs. Peacock, who was so angry and flustered after her wild cab ride that she had completely forgotten the time. She marched furiously toward the Boddy front door, shouting over her shoulder to the cab driver, "I'm calling the police. There ought to be a law against drivers like you."

Miss Scarlet completely ignored Mrs. Peacock and touched up her makeup on schedule. Unfortunately, she dropped her tube of lipstick, and it rolled off the drive into the hedge and out of sight.

"Oh, darn," she said, looking around for someone to help her find it. Miss Scarlet spied Colonel Mustard, who had just stabled Sergeant and was walking to the front door. "Excuse me, Colonel dear, I've got a teensy-weensy problem. I've dropped my lipstick and I'm afraid if I try to get it, I'll ruin my nails or, even worse, get a run in my stockings. Would you help me, please?"

The chivalrous Colonel spent five minutes crawling around in the hedge searching for Miss Scarlet's lipstick. Then he remembered his schedule and stood up abruptly. "Sorry, my dear, I really must be going."

Five minutes later, Miss Scarlet cried, "Found it!" She tucked it into her purse and ran for the door.

Mr. Green arrived as planned and promptly locked his emerald-green Porsche. Before he could take a step toward the mansion, his ears were suddenly assaulted by a deafening *Ah-oo-ga!*

Green spun around in time to see Professor Plum, who had just stepped out of his student's car, stumble into Mr. Green's Porsche. "Now look what you've done," Green snapped at the Professor. "You've set off my car alarm."

"Sorry, old man," the Professor apologized. "But my purple mortarboard flew off and I was attempting to retrieve it. Unfortunately it seems to be stuck under your car. Could you, by any chance, pull up a little?"

Ten minutes passed as Mr. Green unlocked his car, leapt into the front seat, and screeched forward ten feet. Plum grabbed for his hat but another sudden gust of wind sent it sailing over the top of the car. Plum chased it toward the front door, leaving Green to reset his car alarm.

In the midst of all this commotion the clock struck twelve, the doorbell was rung, and the winner received the just reward.

## WHO ARRIVED AT THE STROKE OF MIDNIGHT?

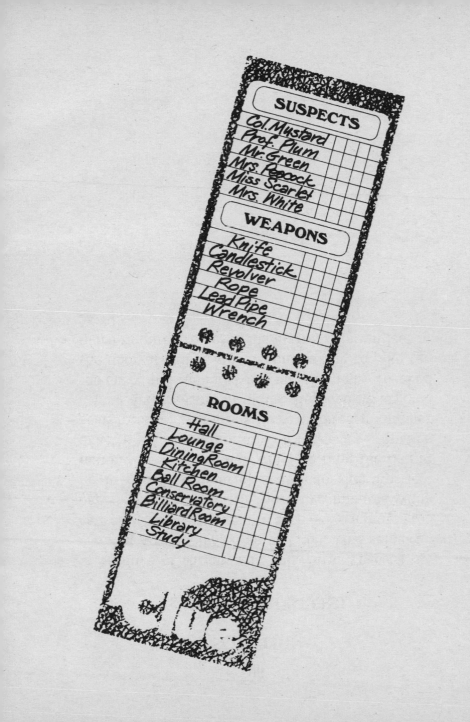

# SOLUTION

## COLONEL MUSTARD

Because of the speedy cab, Mrs. Peacock arrived at Mr. Boddy's door at 11:50. That same cab caused Colonel Mustard to arrive five minutes too early. But he made up those five minutes when he helped Miss Scarlet search for her lipstick, making him the winner when he rang the bell at exactly 12:00 midnight. Miss Scarlet's lipstick search continued for five more minutes, giving her a final arrival time of 12:05. Because he arrived too early and then lost his hat, Plum also reached the door at 12:05. Mr. Green, having to take ten more minutes to reset his alarm, came in last at 12:20.

# 10.
# The Clue in the Shadows

"**I** wish this rain would stop," Miss Scarlet complained as she looked out the Library window Saturday morning. The guests had only just arrived for the weekend and already were going a little stir-crazy.

"It'll never stop," Mr. Green announced in his gloomiest voice. "It was raining on Thursday, it poured all day Friday, and I'm certain this downpour shall continue throughout our entire stay."

"Yes," Mrs. Peacock sighed heavily. "I had to leave my luggage in the front Hall to dry. It was simply too soggy to take up to my room."

"I did the same with mine," Professor Plum said.

"Mine is dripping away next to Plum's," added Colonel Mustard.

Miss Scarlet, who couldn't bear to hear one more word about soggy luggage, flopped on the couch and announced dramatically, "I'm bored! Let's *do something*."

Mr. Boddy hated seeing his guests so miserable. "Why don't we play a game?" he suggested.

"A board game!" Miss Scarlet said, smiling for the first time since she'd arrived dripping wet on the front steps of the Boddy mansion.

"Why would she want to play a bored game when she's already bored?" mused Professor Plum, shuffling to the couch in his purple slippers (which he was wearing because his shoes were soaked).

"Don't be so daft," murmured Mrs. White, who had brought everyone steaming mugs of hot chocolate to take the chill off.

"How about anagrams?" suggested Mr. Boddy.

"Anna-what?" asked Mrs. Peacock, who hadn't realized she was wearing a whipped-cream mustache from sipping her chocolate.

Mrs. White noticed it first but wasn't about to tell her. She just chuckled merrily from her position by the tray of cookies on the side table.

"Ana*grams*," repeated Mr. Boddy, checking his own lip to make sure he didn't have a mustache like Mrs. Peacock's. "You try to unscramble scrambled words. For example, one of you here is a lump."

"A lump?" said Mrs. Peacock, setting her mug down on the table. "How rude!"

"He means Plum," said Mrs. White, figuring it out. (She loved word games.) "Lump is Plum, scrambled."

"And Colonel Mustard," said Mr. Boddy, pointing at the mustachioed military man with a

92

mischievous grin, "I challenge you to a leud!"

"You do?" Mustard leapt to his feet and pulled out his sword. "Challenge accepted." Just as quickly he lowered the sword, completely befuddled. "What's a leud?"

"A duel, you fool!" cried Mrs. Peacock, who had by now caught on that she had a silly mustache and was determined to make someone else feel equally ridiculous. "Leud is an anagram for duel. And a very rude one, I must add."

"In that case," huffed Colonel Mustard as he pointed his sword her way, "I challenge *you* to a leud."

"I think I get it now," said Miss Scarlet. She clasped her hands together and spoke in an exaggerated tone. "You might say that I love *erd.*"

"You mean *red*," Mr. Green shouted happily. He had been seriously worried that he was going to be the only one who hadn't figured it out. Now he took a loud slurp of his hot chocolate in celebration (taking care, of course, not to get a mustache like Mrs. Peacock).

"Yes, I think we all *stundernad*," Professor Plum said with a coy smile.

"Stundernad?" Mr. Boddy cocked his head to the side. "Ah! *Understand*. Jolly good."

Despite the downpour outside the Library window, the group was now feeling positively giddy. Boddy strode over to the bookshelf and, taking down his anagram board and letters, set it on the coffee table.

Miss Scarlet leapt to her feet. "I get to pick my letters first."

"No, *I* do," Mr. Green said. "You always go first."

Miss Scarlet narrowed her eyes at him. "I do not."

"Do too," Colonel Mustard replied, joining the fray.

"Do not," shouted Miss Scarlet, spinning to face him.

"Do too!" the Colonel roared back.

Mr. Boddy quickly ran to his gaming cupboard and pulled out a referee's whistle.

*Tweet!*

Colonel Mustard snapped to attention. Mrs. White winced. Mr. Green scowled. Miss Scarlet stuck her fingers in her ears. Mrs. Peacock jumped in alarm, spilling her chocolate. And Professor Plum, who thought it was his own hearing aid shorting out, tilted his head to one side and banged on it several times with his hand.

"Listen up!" Mr. Boddy ordered. "I can't stand this endless bickering. To make sure it doesn't happen anymore today, I'll give a gold coin to each player who makes it through this game without fighting or arguing."

Miss Scarlet dropped her hands from her ears. "Gold coins?"

"Yes." Mr. Boddy took a blue velvet box from one of the Library shelves. Nestled snugly inside it were six dazzling gold coins.

"Rare Spanish doubloons," he said, passing them around the group. "From Ponce De Leon's own treasure chest."

"Ooooooh!"

The guests were very impressed. They all wished that they had investigated the contents of the box and discovered the gold coins. They all started scheming.

Mr. Boddy scooped the rare gold coins out of the box and dropped them into his inside coat pocket. "Shall we begin?"

The guests nodded meekly.

Five minutes later . . .

Five minutes later, they were well into the first round of their anagram game. Mr. Boddy was perplexed. On the one hand, the guests were being very careful not to argue. But they seemed oddly distracted and unable to concentrate.

Mr. Boddy suspected that the reason for their distraction was that each one was feverishly trying to figure out how to steal *all* of the gold coins. As a precaution, he took the coins out of his pocket and put them in the blue velvet box while the others were involved in playing anagrams. He placed the box high on a shelf and quietly returned to the game.

Suddenly a loud crash came from the front Hall.

"Mrs. White, see to that, will you?" Mr. Boddy asked. "It sounded like the roof just fell in."

Mrs. White hurried into the Hall and returned after several minutes. This time she was clad in a white slicker raincoat and squeaking white rubber boots. Water dripped off her matching slicker hat.

"Well?" Mr. Boddy asked.

"You were right, sir. The roof *did* just fall in."

"My word! Where?"

"In the front Hall." A slow smile crept across Mrs. White's lips. "The part just above the drying luggage."

The guests instantly bolted for the Library door. But the second they reached the door, everyone froze. You see, they wanted to save their luggage, but they also wanted to get at the gold coins.

"My red canvas purse," Miss Scarlet cried. "It has all my makeup and accessories. I must save it."

Mrs. White was the only one who saw Miss Scarlet grab a weapon on her way out of the room. It flashed in the Library light before being tucked inside Miss Scarlet's red angora sweater.

"My blue tapestry bag." Mrs. Peacock slyly slipped a Revolver into her pocket. "I must save my knitting."

Not wanting to be unarmed herself, Mrs. White picked up a glinting metal implement and dropped it into her apron.

"My yellow duffel bag," shouted Mustard, grasping a blunt metal object firmly behind him as he backed out of the room. "I must go retrieve it. The duffel contains all my medals and citations for bravery."

"My purple briefcase," said Plum, tucking a shiny object into his coat. "I must get it. It holds every academic paper I've ever written."

"I've got my green valise with all my important business papers." Mr. Green grabbed a Rope but, having no place to hide it, held it up for Mr. Boddy and Mrs. White to see. "I'll just take this Rope, in case we need it to drag the luggage out of the rain."

After Mr. Green left the room, Mrs. White turned to Mr. Boddy and said, "I'll just see what I can do to help."

Mr. Boddy was left alone in the Library.

Since the game was at a standstill, he decided he might as well take this opportunity to call the plumber. He crossed to the phone resting on the mahogany table and dialed.

"Hello?" Mr. Boddy spoke into the receiver. "I need to speak with Mr. Sprocket. Yes. Well, it *is* an emergency. . . . All right, I'll hold."

While he was waiting for Mr. Sprocket to come to the phone, Boddy heard the tap-tap sound of shoes on the wooden floor behind him. His eyes widened as he saw on the wall the shadow of an arm being raised.

"What the — ?" Boddy turned and gasped but was silenced instantly. He slumped to the ground, barely conscious.

The person who had tiptoed back into the room rifled through Mr. Boddy's pockets. When no coins were discovered, the intruder began searching the room frantically.

"Help! Somebody help!" Mr. Boddy called from where he lay on the floor. He could tell that his voice was too weak to be heard by anyone in the Hall. There was only one thing left to do.

Slowly, he crawled to the anagram board and spelled out the following message:

FIKEN RILYBAR

But before he could finish writing, he collapsed. For good.

Meanwhile, the intruder found the gold coins and was making off with them just as some of the other guests burst into the Library. All they saw was the back of the figure retreating into the shadows and disappearing into the secret passage.

WHO KILLED BODDY? WITH WHAT? WHERE?

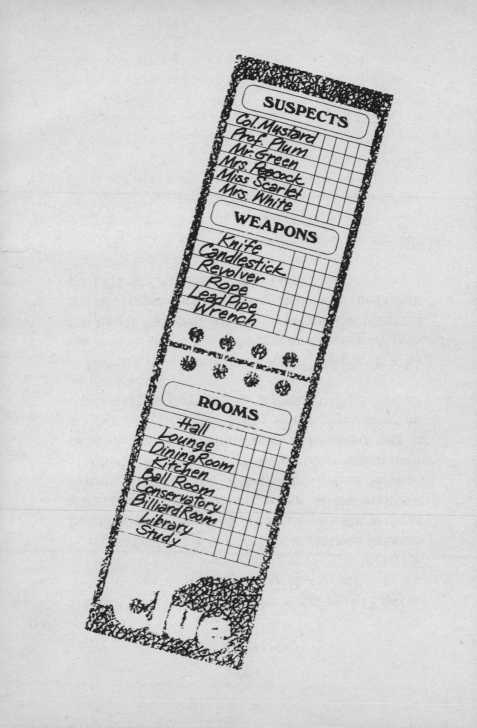

# SOLUTION

## MISS SCARLET with the KNIFE (FIKEN) in the LIBRARY (RILYBAR)

We know that Mr. Boddy was stabbed because he spelled the anagram for Knife. We know three guests took shiny weapons out of the room — White, Scarlet, and Plum. Just before he was stabbed, Boddy heard shoes on the wooden floor behind him. That eliminated Plum, who was in slippers. We know Mrs. White was wearing squeaking rubber boots, so that left Miss Scarlet as the culprit.

Luckily, the Knife missed Mr. Boddy, but he decided to teach his rude guests a lesson by pretending to be dead. After they solved the anagram puzzle, they noticed two more words on the board: PALIR SLOOF, or April Fools.